THIS BOOK BELONGS TO

_____

I'm Your Child, God

GOD

Prayers for Our Children

Marian Wright Edelman

Illustrated by

Bryan Collier

HYPERION BOOKS FOR CHILDREN

NEW YORK

First Edition
1 3 5 7 9 10 8 6 4 2
Printed in Hong Kong
This book is set in 16-point Deepdene.

Library of Congress Cataloging-in-Publication Data on file.

ISBN 0-7868-0597-8 (trade)

Visit www.hyperionchildrensbooks.com

To my granddaughter, Ellika Amie,
and to all the children and grandchildren of the world now and to come
for whom we hold the present and future in trust.
I pray that one day our nation and our world will get God's message
that it is the child who is God's messenger of love and hope
for the future, and commit to leaving not a single child behind.

—M.W.E.

To all the children of the world.
Always remember in every moment
to look out for the pieces of the puzzle.

—B.C.

ILLUSTRATOR'S NOTE

This text will speak to you on so many different levels, no matter what age you are.

In the artwork, you will see vertical bands of color in the faces of the children, symbolizing blessings falling upon them. The bands of color also reflect our oneness with everyone, no matter what color we are.

The biggest gift that I walk away with is that everything that happens to you on a moment-to-moment basis is like receiving a piece of a puzzle. You examine the odd-shaped piece without knowing where it fits in your life. I believe you should hold on to that odd-shaped piece, because the blessing of God's divine plan is that all those puzzle pieces begin to form something that is whole and complete—the miracle that is you.

—B.C.

ACKNOWLEDGMENTS

I am grateful for the beautiful spaces to be silent and to write provided by my friends
Deborah Szekely and Carol and Frank Biondi.
Special thanks to Martha Espinosa for her patient and thoughtful assistance and to
Shannon Daley-Harris and Lisa Clayton Robinson for their careful reading of this book.
I feel privileged to have Bryan Collier as illustrator of this book.

—M.W.E.

Special thanks to my editor, Maureen Sullivan

—B.C.

Guide my feet while I run this race,
    for I don't want to run this race in vain.
I'm Your child while I run this race,
    for I don't want to run this race in vain.
Search my heart while I run this race,
    for I don't want to run this race in vain.
Stand by me while I run this race,
    for I don't want to run this race in vain.
Hold my hand while I run this race,
    for I don't want to run this race in vain.
                  —*Negro Spiritual*

CONTENTS

PREFACE

T HIS IS MY THIRD BOOK OF PRAYERS. The first, *Guide My Feet: Prayers and Meditations on Loving and Working for Children*, was written for adults who love, care for, and serve individual children. The second, *Hold My Hand: Prayers for Building a Movement to Leave No Child Behind*, was written to give courage and strength to those willing to go beyond their daily loving service for individual children to advocacy, mobilization, and organizing for all children, to ensure that our rich and powerful nation *truly* leaves no child behind. This book is for children, who need stronger inner anchors and spiritual grounding in our too materialistic, too violent, too busy, too noisy, too secular, and too individualistic, fragile, and ever-changing nation and world, where ties to family, community, and the sacred are becoming increasingly frayed.

A number of the prayers in this book arise out of the needs of children suffering economic and/or emotional poverty. These are children in every race, income group, family type, and place in America. Contrary to popular stereotype, a poor child in America is more likely to be White than Black or Latino; is more likely to live in a rural or suburban area than in an inner city; and is much more likely to live in a working family than to be on welfare. Over 7 million of our nearly 12 million poor children are White. Many more White than minority children get pregnant, take drugs, and get killed by guns every year. *Affluenza*—a poverty of values, purpose, and integrity—afflicts millions of nonpoor children who are as adrift and in need of family guidance and supports as many poor children.

As a child and teenager, I prayed a lot in gratitude for the blessings of parents and a sister and brothers who loved me, and for home and church and neighbors and community people who cared about me. Prayer helped me through some very tough times—my father's death when I was fourteen years old; when I was teased because I had skinny legs and a big nose; was put down or ignored because I was a girl; or was heckled, called bad names, and treated unfairly because I am Black. When I disappointed myself and others who cared about me, I prayed for forgiveness and help to do better. Too often I prayed, when I'd done something wrong, not to get caught—promising never to do it again if God would save me still one more time! When I couldn't talk to anyone else, I could always share with God what I was feeling.

I have written all of the prayers in this book except for a few of the favorite prayers and passages from the Bible and the graces in the last chapter, many of which I learned at home during childhood. I have tried to pass some of them on to my sons, who I pray will pass them on to their children and their children's children. Included are prayers for happy, sad, hopeful, confused, joyful, scary, and lonely times, and for difficult family changes like a divorce, a move, and the death of a family member, friend, or pet. Some prayers celebrate important transitions and occasions. Some are for children who do not have families, whose lives are as fragile as the thinnest thread—bruised, battered, bothered, and abused by physical and emotional homelessness, hunger, neglect, and gun violence inflicted against them by their families, neighbors, and others in a nation where it is safer to be an on-duty law enforcement officer than a child under ten.

These prayers are just a beginning for what I hope will become a lifelong conversation between children and God.

Prayer exercises the spirit and nourishes the soul just as food nourishes the body and thought the mind. Prayer can be an attitude of gratitude—a thank-you for life and all its gifts and challenges. Prayer can be an urgent cry or a gentle request for help. Prayer is always hope for or belief in a presence beyond the self that is a source of love, help, guidance, and companionship along life's path.

Prayer has no boundaries of form or place or faith. It is as boundless as God's love and mercy, as big as the human spirit, and as wide as the earth. Prayer is listening and talking and being open to God. It can be silent, spoken, breathed, written, sung, sighed, cried, screamed, dreamed, danced, walked, or thought; and it can be so much more than words can ever express. Prayer can mean being active, being still, being present, being silent. Just being. Prayer can be individual, personal, private or collective; spontaneous or part of age-old rituals and celebrations. It can be unceasing, continuous, or sporadic. It is always good, for it says, *I remember there is something bigger than I am. I acknowledge the Creator of life.*

I hope the prayers in this book will strengthen, comfort, and bring joyful soul food and encouragement to children in their quest for the meaning of life as they journey on.

—M.W.E.

A PARENT'S AND GRANDPARENT'S CREDO OF FAITH, LOVE, HOPE, STRENGTH, CARING, AND SERVICE FOR EVERY CHILD

This book is a credo of faith I wish for every child:

O my children, I know and testify that God lives because
I've heard Martin Luther King, Jr.,
   and Fred Shuttlesworth preach;
I've heard Aretha Franklin, Marian Anderson,
   and Pavarotti sing;
I've seen double rainbows after the storm,
and the sun come up and go down
in blazes of color no words can describe.
I've pondered the purple iris and the smiling sunflower
and smelled the sweet rose;
stood as a speck before majestic mountains
and listened in awe to the ocean's roar;
experienced the miracles of birth,
the gratitude of parenthood and grandparenthood,
and the joy of children's love and laughter.
O my children, I know that God lives
because God created you.

This book is a credo of love for every sacred and special child of God:

Black and Brown girl dark of hue with kinky hair,
God painted your skin and curled your hair just for you.
God is love and you are God's beloved.

Black, Brown, Yellow, Red, White, and those all-mixed-together child
created to look just like you,
God rejoices and is glad in you.
God is love and you are God's beloved.

Special child who sees and discerns and navigates
without the eyes or ears or
hands or legs others need,
God is love and you are God's beloved.

Weary child of the night and of the streets,
afraid and abused and in need of safe haven and home
to rest and to nest,
God is love and you are God's beloved.

Child of slow mind, innocent of worldly wiles

and the will to harm others,

freed of devious thoughts the sinful of mind like me so often display,

God is love and you are God's beloved.

Child of poverty unburdened by the chains of things

and greed that imprison the have-too-muches,

God came in your disguise to save us all.

God is love and you are God's beloved.

This book is a credo of hope that our children and grandchildren
will feel empowered to build a more just and peaceful world.

O God, help our children and grandchildren

to feel love and appreciation for all Your gifts of life.

Grant each of them a passion for peace and for justice.

Kindness for those who are weak and needy and sad and afraid.

Courage to stand up for right and to struggle against wrong.

Friendship and kinship with all who share the world You have created.

Grant our children faith to open the door of their souls

and to live their lives as You intend.

Protect them against the worms of hate

and the weasels of selfishness and envy.

Help our children to sing their own songs

and to hear and join in the songs of others

in the spheres of the earth's firmament.

**This book is a credo of strength, celebrating the capacity
of the human spirit, in children, to beat the odds.**

Live, child—no matter what!
Don't let anybody or anything stop you.
Like the flowers in the crannied walls
squeezing life as ivy, fern, molds, and yellow buds
stretching toward the sun
rise from the rocky soil
cling to the naked bumpy walls
work your roots into the tiny crevices, nooks, and crannies of the unfriendly
walls of race and class and gender that try to block your way.
Live no matter what
lapping up sun's warmth and rain's drops
bend with the wind and dance with the breeze
crawl up and down and all around
cover the stone walls with your green coverlet
going on with your life.

**This book is a credo of caring and service enabling every child
to know that they can serve and make a difference.**

Lord, I cannot preach like Martin Luther King, Jr.,
or turn a poetic phrase like Maya Angelou,
but I care and am willing to serve.

I do not have Harriet Tubman's courage
or Franklin and Eleanor Roosevelt's political skills,
but I care and am willing to serve.

I cannot sing like Fannie Lou Hamer
or organize like Bayard Rustin,
but I care and am willing to serve.

I am not holy like Archbishop Desmond Tutu,
forgiving like Nelson Mandela,
or disciplined like Mahatma Gandhi,
but I care and am willing to serve.

I am not brilliant like Elizabeth Cady Stanton
and George Washington Carver,
or as eloquent as Sojourner Truth and Booker T. Washington,
but I care and am willing to serve.

I have not Mother Teresa's saintliness,
Dorothy Day's love or Cesar Chavez's
gentle tough spirit,
but I care and am willing to serve.

God, it is not as easy as it used to be
to frame an issue and to forge a solution,
but I care and am willing to serve.

I can't see or hear well or speak good English,
I stutter sometimes, am afraid of criticism,
and get really scared standing up before others,
but I care and am willing to serve.

I'm so young,
nobody will listen.
I'm not sure what to say or do,
but I care and am willing to serve.

God, use me as Thou will today and tomorrow
to help build a nation and world
where no child is left behind
and everyone feels welcome.

I'm Your Child, God

Prayers for Our Children

PRAYERS
FOR
YOUNGER CHILDREN

MORNING PRAYERS

O God, who created the sun and the moon
and the stars and the seas and my family,
Thank You for creating me.

Good morning, sun.
Good morning, sky.
Good morning, Mommy.
Good morning, Daddy.
Good morning, everybody.
Good morning, God.
Thank You for a new day.

God, I love You.
God, I trust You.
God, I'm so happy You love me too.

I love my mommy
and my mommy loves me.
God bless my mommy
and God bless me.

I love my daddy
and my daddy loves me.
God bless my daddy
and God bless me.

I love my brother/sister/grandma/grandpa
and my brother/sister/grandma/grandpa loves me.
God bless my brother/sister/grandma/grandpa
and God bless me.

God, please help me to be kind to other people
and help other people to be kind to me.

6

A CHILD'S PRAYER FOR A PARENT
LEAVING HOME FOR WORK

Good-bye, Mommy
Good-bye, Daddy
God bless your day at work
and bring you home safe and soon.

A CHILD'S PRAYER ON LEAVING
FOR SCHOOL

Good-bye, Mommy
Good-bye, Daddy
I am off to school to learn and play
I'll see you later in the day
and pray God keeps me good and safe.

FOR A PARENT'S RETURN

My mom and dad went to visit
friends who live far away.
I hope that they will come back soon
since I will miss them so.
God keep them safe wherever they go
and bring them back home to me.

PROTECTION

From ghosts and goblins
and snakes under the bed,
please deliver me, God.

From guns and gangs
and big scary things,
please protect me, God.

From bullies and bad people
who tease and abuse and make me afraid,
please keep me safe, God.

From those who don't see or hear me
or care whether I exist,
please shield me, God.

From doubt and despair
and the low expectations of others,
please lift me, God.

HOPE

God, help me to let my little light
shine every day and
every night and everywhere I go
so that there will always be a light in the world.

God, where did I come from?
Where am I going?
What do You want me to be?
Are You there?

Dear God,
I feel like a little caterpillar today
but I know I'll be a beautiful butterfly tomorrow
and fly toward the sky.

I talk to God and God talks to me
in the pitter-patter of the rain and in the whistle of the wind
and in the gurgle of the brook.
I smile at God and God smiles back at me
in the faces of the pansy, the sunflower, and the man on the moon.
I sing to God and God sings to me
through the mockingbird and the lark and the cooing dove too.
I dance for God and God dances for me
in the swaying of the trees and the ripples in the pond.
I pray to God and God prays for me
through the grace of the saints and of those who pray for others.

O God, light a candle in my heart
and sweep the darkness from Your dwelling space.
Amen.

Dear Lord,
Help me to become
who You want me to be.
Amen.

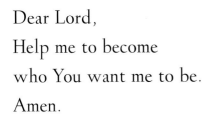

God, I wish I were a tugboat
pulling big ships out to sea.
I wish I were a big airplane
taking people to faraway places.
I wish I were a great big fish
and could roam the sea at will.
I wish I were an eagle
who could fly and touch the sky.
I wish I were an angel
who shuttles between heaven and earth.
I wish I were a fairy
who could wipe away famine with my wand.
I wish I were good like You and
could love everyone I see.

PRAYER FOR ATTENTION

Invisible me
who nobody sees
except when I act up.

Invisible me
who nobody listens to
unless I scream and holler.

Invisible me
who nobody talks to
until I get in trouble.

The good me is silent
the bad me is loud
I wish I were a cloud.

SERVICE

Dear Lord,
Help me to be a blessing to someone today.

Dear Lord,
Help me to be Your
hands, feet, eyes,
ears, and voice in the world today.

Dear Lord,
Help others in my family
and in my school to see and feel
You in me today.

Thank You, Lord, for another
day of life.
Bless it to Your service and glory.

God, my hands are small,
but I can help
in many ways.
My legs are not long,

but I can run an errand
for an elderly or sick
neighbor who can't.

My voice is not as loud as others
but I can sing a soothing melody and cheer a heart.

Thank You, God, for making me useful.

GRATITUDE

A buzzy bee came to eat—
what was I to do?
I let him have a bite or two—
then he was content too.
Thank You, God, for food to eat and to share.

Dear Lord,
Help me to live right now
in this moment of time
You have given me.

Thank You, Lord
Forgive me, Lord
Help me, Lord
Save me, Lord.

Thank You, God, for this perfect day of life.

O God, I am only a little child but I feel Your love everywhere
in the sunlight that warms my face
in the breeze that wraps around my arms
in the songs of birds praising the day
in green trees and leaves swaying in the wind.
Thank You for sharing all these blessings with me,
Your child.

Thank You, Jesus, for loving children
and for wanting to be with us.
Thank You, Jesus, for welcoming children
when others turn us away.
Thank You, Jesus, for praising children
as trusting and loving and good.
Thank You, Jesus, for coming to earth
as a child to bless us all.

Dear Lord,
Thank You for my mother.
Thank You for my father.
Thank You for my grandparents.

Thank You for my sister and my brother.
Thank You for my aunts and uncles.
Thank You for my friends.
Thank You for the sun and moon.
Thank You for the dewdrops and
     the stars so bright.
Thank You that Mama did not
     serve peas or broccoli tonight.

Dear Lord,
I thank You for my friend
who never lets me down
who accepts me as I am
and expects the same of me.

Dear Lord,
I thank You for my grandmother,
who's always there for me.
She smiles and soothes my feelings
when they get hurt
and lets me stay up late.

Thank You, God, for being my friend
for loving me all the time
and never leaving me alone.
I love You too.
And I like having You to talk to.

O God, who never saw a child too bad to love
too sinful to forgive
too lost to be found.
Thank You for loving and never giving up
on any child you have made, including me.

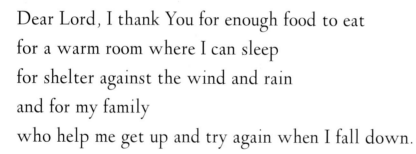

Dear Lord, I thank You for enough food to eat
for a warm room where I can sleep
for shelter against the wind and rain
and for my family
who help me get up and try again when I fall down.

Lord, You made me a girl and I am so proud.
Some people think I'm not as
good or as smart or as useful as a boy.
but You and I know they are wrong.
Thank You for making me who I am.
Help me to make You proud of me and to be all that I can be
despite what the world may say.

NEW SIBLING

Dear God,
When I have a new baby brother or sister
will Mommy and Daddy love him or her more than me?

Suppose she's prettier,
suppose he's cuter.
Will they still love me as much as before?

20

PEACE

I pray for peace
in myself
in my family
in my community
in my country
and in all the world.

I pray that no one will hate
that no one will kill
that all will forgive
and live in love.

Lord,
Please stop the violence and wars that kill children.
Help us to love each other and to live together in peace.

Dear Lord,
You have blessed me with so much.
Please help me help children
who do not have enough to eat
or a place to sleep.

Dear God,
Help me to help make a better world
for all children everywhere
where none go hungry
or are unsafe
or have to cry in fear.

Help me to help make a better world
where every child feels loved
and none is left behind because nobody cares.

Help me to help make a better world
where bombs don't drop at all
and guns are buried in the earth
and land mines don't exist,
so children can play and grow.

FEAR OF THE DARK

Dear God,
I am so afraid of the dark.
Please bring the morning soon.

BEDTIME PRAYERS

Good night, God
Thank You for today.
I'll see You tomorrow.
Please watch over me while I sleep.

All day, all night,
please send Your angels, God,
to watch over me.
Amen.

—*From a Negro Spiritual*

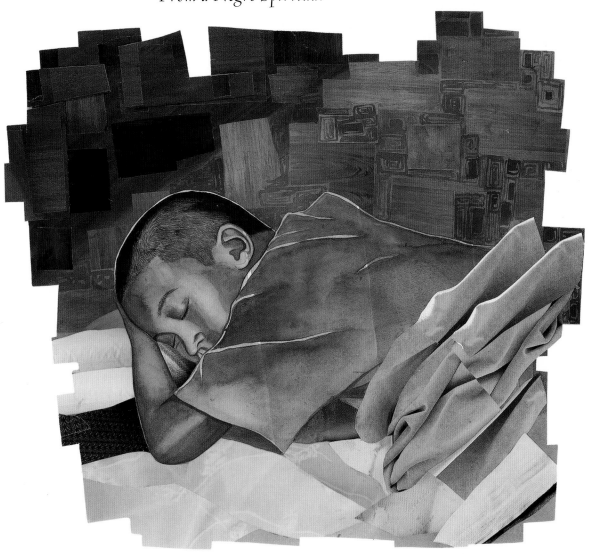

Dear God,
I am about to go to sleep.
Please hold me safe in Your arms
until morning comes.

O God,
Help me to shine like the sun
glow like the moon
play peekaboo like the stars
dance like the rain
and bring joy and smiles
to all I meet.

The sun shines every day
the moon shines every night
the stars twinkle and shine all over the sky
even when I cannot see them.
Thank You, God, that
You are always there
every day and every night
everywhere.

Prayers for Older Children

GUIDANCE

I asked God,
"What do You want me to be?"

God replied,
"Whatever you want to be
with the talents and life I gave you.
I believe in you and want you to believe in yourself
and in my good plans for you."

God, You used David to slay the giant Goliath
when he was just a boy
and when all of King Saul's army was afraid.

You appointed young Jeremiah a prophet to the nations
and commanded him to speak and not to be afraid.

Esther was a mere teenage girl when You gave her courage
to ask the king to save her people.

You called Samuel in the middle of the night
as he lay in the temple,
and he answered: "Speak, for Thy servant hears."

Speak to me, Lord, for I want to be Your servant, too.

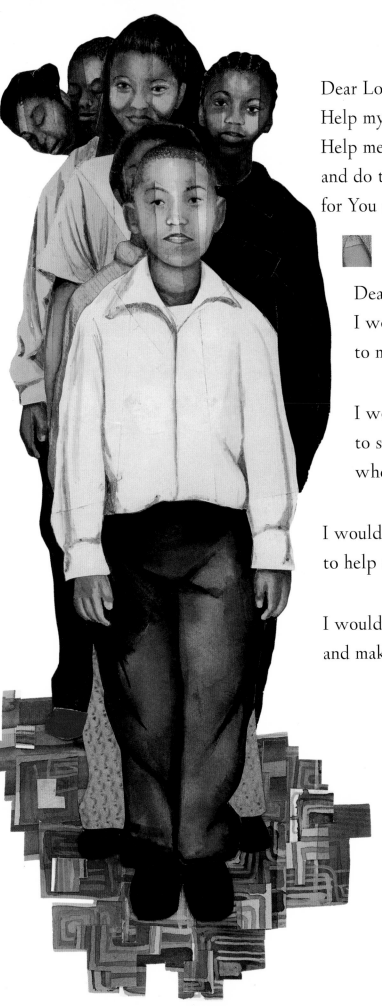

Dear Lord,
Help my life to be real and true
Help me to be the best that I can be
and do the best that I can do
for You and my family and community.

Dear God,
I would like to be a doctor
to make people well.

I would like to be a lawyer
to seek justice for all people
when they are in trouble.

I would like to be a teacher
to help all children learn.

I would like to be a good child
and make my parents proud.

2 9

Dear God,
Help me to place my trust and make my home in You
and to make You welcome in the home of my soul.

Dear God,
Please tell me who You want me to be
and what You want me to do
and help me be and do what You want.

God, help me to
Feel. Sing. Dance. Ask. See. Laugh. Learn. Dare. Act. Be.

Dear God,
Help me to give and not just to take
to do and not just to talk
to pray and to work
to be a "go-giver" and a "go-getter."

What do You want me to do today, Lord?

O God,
Open my eyes, my ears, and my heart that I may see, hear, and feel
Your presence in myself and in everyone I meet today.

O Lord, light a candle in my heart
so I can help someone else see their way.

Dear God,
Help me to share my love with others
as You have shared Your love with me.

Help me to share my talents with others
as You have given them to me.

Help me to share my joy with others
as life is full of joy.

God,
I want to be a doctor when I grow up,
but my counselor says I can't.
She says I'm not smart enough
and ought to think more realistically.
I know my tests are not the best,
but I'm willing to work harder to realize my dream.
Will You help me, Lord?

FORGIVENESS

O God, who hears and sees everything I think and do, forgive.
O God, whose grace is as bountiful as the air, forgive.
O God, whose mercy is as wide as the sea, forgive.
O God, whose faithfulness is as high as the sky, forgive.
O God, who will always hear me and help me, thank You.

O God,
I did not mean to hurt my mother or make my little brother cry.
He's such a pest.
I needed a rest
and wanted to be alone.
Next time I'll do better and find a secret place
where I can read in peace.

I cheated on my test today
because I did not want to fail.
I was afraid my parents would punish me.
Lord, now I'm afraid You will.
Please forgive me and help me not to cheat again.

PROTECTION

Where are You, Lord? Come by here.
I'm afraid I'm going to get shot.
I'm afraid my mama's going to get shot.
I'm afraid my daddy's going to get shot.
I'm afraid my brother won't come home.
I'm afraid of the gangs that roam my street and drug dealers who
     are everywhere,
I'm afraid of the knives and guns at school.
I'm afraid of the rats and roaches at home.
I'm afraid of being beaten when I wake up.
I'm afraid of the violence around me all the time.
I'm afraid I won't get to grow up at all.
I'm afraid You don't love me—that nobody does.
I'm afraid, God.
Please let me live.

Dear Lord,
Go with me today
everywhere I go, and with my family, too.
Wrap us in Your kind blanket of care
and keep us all safe as we go on our way.

God,
My friend got shot today.
It could have been me.
There's no place to hide from death
in my street or school or home.
How long will it take for good people
to stop innocent children
from being killed for no reason?

SERVICE

I thank You for all the people
who make our country great—
who grow food to eat, build houses where people can sleep
and make clothes that keep us warm
who clean the schools we learn in, the parks we play in
and the streets we walk on
who drive the buses and trains that take us where we have to go
and protect us from dangers of all kinds

who heal us when we are sick
and teach us what we need to know
who provide jobs for our parents, who work for justice in our country,
and who vote to elect and who try to be good leaders.
Thank You, God, for all who make America great.

I thank You, God, for the great cloud of witnesses
who went before me to prepare my way today
who overcame slavery and battled segregation and
worked to free our nation from the yoke of racism.
Help me never to forget what they did for me and for all of us
and help me to carry on the never-ending struggle
for freedom and justice and peace for all.

GRATITUDE

God, my friend and mother and father,
Nobody ever writes me a letter.
Nobody ever gives me a present.
Nobody ever takes me to the beach or the zoo.
Nobody reads me Dr. Seuss.
Nobody ever gives me surprises.
Nobody ever wakes me up to see the sunrise.
Nobody tells me about fairies and princesses.
Nobody shares their dreams and asks me mine.

Nobody reminds me to look up at the sky.
Nobody greets me with a cheery good morning
or kisses me sweetly as I fall asleep.
Nobody cares when I come or go, or whether I am happy or sad,
or if I live or die.
Nobody but You, God.
Thank You for being my friend.

Thank You, God, for everyone in my family.
Thank You, God, for everyone in my community
who tries to love and help others.
Thank You, God, for everyone in the world
who works for peace and justice and a better life for all.

Dear God,
I pray for faith when life gets difficult.
I pray for hope even though I do not feel it.
I pray for love when hate raises its ugly face.
I pray for the joy that comes from You,
knowing the life You have given me is a gift of great good.

RESPECT

Lord, please help people not to
see me as a shadow
of my mother and father.
I have my own light.
I have my own mind.
I have my own dreams.
I have my own gifts.
Please help others to see
and to let me be me.

Dear God,
Please tell my parents, teachers,
and the adults I meet
to respect me,
pay attention to me,
and be kind to me.

O God,
I can never seem to do enough
to please my mother and father.
I try so hard and possibly shouldn't bother.
They never applaud what I have done
but always remember what I don't do.
Tell them my efforts should count as well as my mistakes.
Help them to encourage me so I can keep trying.

God,
A boy called me nigger
and then started to snicker.
I wondered who taught him how
to hurt and hate this way.
I pray that he will learn better
as he grows older
so that America can become better,
and children can grow to respect one another.

FEAR

O God,
I'm so afraid I'm going to fail in school.
Please help me not to give up.
I can't concentrate.
My teacher's losing patience.
Please send me the help I need to succeed.

O Lord, help!
I'm going to flunk my test.
I may flunk my grade.
I don't want to be held back.
I don't want my friends to think I am dumb.
I don't want my parents to be angry.
I don't want to keep falling behind.
I want to do well in school but I need help.
Will You help me ask for help now
or send someone who sees my need, Lord?

DEATH

O God,
Someone I love died today.
I pray You will wrap him in your arms and wipe his pain away.
I'll miss him so but know he's secure in the love of You who made him.
Tell him I love him and will try hard to be as good as he taught
me to be when he was here.
Grant to his soul peace and eternal rest.

DEATH OF A PET

God,
My pet died today.
I cried and cried and felt so bad.
Is there a pet heaven God?
Is it the same for people?
Will we see each other again?
I hope so.

FAMILY STRUGGLES

Please help my daddy come home.
I miss him so much.
I don't want him to be sick.
I'm so scared he'll die.
Please help him to be all right and to come home soon.

Where are You, Lord?
My mother is sick,
and I am so afraid.
I won't have anybody to
care for me.
I love her so very much.
Please don't take her from me.
I need her, Lord.
Please make her well again

O Lord,
My mommy and my daddy don't love each other anymore.
They fight all the time and say bad things about each other.
I am so afraid.
I don't want to choose.
I love them both.
Will they leave me if they leave each other?
Lord, I don't want to lose my mommy.

I don't want to lose my daddy.
I don't want to lose my home.
I don't want to go back and forth
from Mommy's to Daddy's house.
I want the home and family I have.
Please help them, Lord, to see how much I need them
to love and protect me and to be kind to each other again.

My mommy and daddy fight all the time.
They tell me bad things about each other.
They say they can't live together anymore because
they don't love each other anymore.

Why do they fight so, Lord?
Is it because I've been bad?
Will they stop loving me too, Lord?

FAITH

God, help me to remember this
when I do not remember anything else:
no matter how sad or scared I am,
You love me so much
that You gave Your only Son to be my friend
to make sure I am never alone.

God, be the master of my home and of my heart.

O God, who makes the impossible possible
who brings morning after night
and tells the waves be still—
give me faith to trust in Your grace
and seek to do Your will.

God will shield me with unfailing faithfulness.
God will swaddle me in ceaseless love
and be with me every step of my way.
Thank You, God.

PRAYERS
FOR
SPECIAL OCCASIONS

GRADUATION

God, I made it!
I'm graduating today from school.
Hallelujah!
Start the party.

I never thought I'd see this day
when I'd walk across this stage.
But by Your grace I've made it through
and made my family proud.

I thank You, God, for this special day made possible
by so many who love me.
My parents, my family, my teachers, and friends
who taught me to care,
to know right from wrong,
and to pray,
I thank You.

A BIRTHDAY PRAYER

Lord,

I thank You for another year of life and growth.

Please help me to seek and find Your purpose for me in life.

Support me so I never give up trying to be a better person.

Help me to see the good in all the people You share with me,

and for them to see and affirm the good in me.

Help me to see how Your love for me shines through

in every experience I have.

THANKSGIVING

O God,

I thank You for this place called home

for family, food, fellowship, and fun

for the freedom to pray, sing, and gather together

to celebrate Your goodness as one.

I thank You for our land and all those who peopled it

for Native Americans who loved, respected and protected the earth

for pilgrims who came in search of freedom to worship

for immigrants who came in search of freedom to speak their beliefs

for those who came against their will but who adopted and worked

to achieve America's dream as their own

for those who tilled the soil, forged the frontiers, built the cities,
cooked and cleaned and raised their families
and held together their communities.
I thank You for all who worked for justice and sacrificed their lives
to make us a freer and better nation.
On this Thanksgiving, I thank You for America and for the dream
of America we must seek to fulfill for all each day.
God bless the world and every child through America.

CHRISTMAS

Christ Jesus, I thank You for coming into the world
as a child like me,
weak yet strong
poor yet rich
full of hope, love, and life,
to be a light for the world.
Born with a purpose
to do God's will.
Help me to be more like You.

It's Christmas Day.

We have no tree.

We have no home of our own.

We have no new toys or clothes.

Mom says the bike and wagon and coat I wanted so much

will have to wait awhile.

But we still have each other.

We sing together.

We pray together.

We hug and love each other.

We are thankful we are alive and

have hope for the future

because of You, our

Savior born today.

HANUKKAH

On this festival of lights,
may each of us let our light shine
for freedom everywhere we go.

PASSOVER

Dear God,
Let us never forget what it means to be free.
Let us never forget what it requires to be free.
Let us fight for freedom for ourselves and others
so that all God's children may be free.

PRAYERS FOR STRUGGLE AND STRENGTH

56

STRENGTH

Lord, I am sad today.
I don't really know why.
Please help me feel better tomorrow.

O God,
Help me to be real.
Help me to be true to You,
To my family, to my friends, to my country, and to myself.
Amen.

Lord, when I do wrong, please set me right.
When I fall down, please lift me up.
When I get lost, please guide my feet back on track.
When I'm weak and tempted to do things I know are wrong,
please give me strength to say no.
When I'm afraid, please hold my hand.

MOVING AND LEAVING FRIENDS

Dear God,
My parents had to move again,
and I had to leave my school.
Every time I begin to feel at ease
it's time to start over again.
I wish I could stay in school
and live in one place all year round
so the teacher could know me
and I could have friends.

FOR A CHILD WHO IS POOR

Dear God,
Christians believe
You came into the world as a poor child.
The world did not know who You were.
It does not know who I am either.
They ignored You.
They ignore me.
What can You do, God,
to help them see You and me?

Jesus, You were born a poor child like me.
Help me and all poor children like You today.
We are hungry and homeless and lonely
and scared and have no good place to lay our heads.
The roaches and rats crawl over the bed I
share with my family members, who push me aside.
One day when I'm big, I'll have a room of my own
without roaches and rats, pokey elbows, and loud snores.

PLEAS FOR HELP

Dear God,
I wish I could find a
hidden treasure and help
my mother pay her bills.

I wish I could invent a special cure so
Daddy wouldn't be sick anymore.

I wish I could wipe a magic potion
all over my body to become
pretty or handsome like others.

I wish I could wave a wand and
banish bad people from the world.

I am so weak, Lord.
Give me Your strength.
I am so afraid, Lord.
Give me Your courage.
I am so confused, Lord.
Give me Your focus.
I am in such a hurry, Lord.
Help me to wait on You.

I want to be good, God,
and not to be bad.
I don't want to take the drugs around me
and wish I could escape them.
I hate the guns which scare me and make people die.
I wish I could banish them but don't know how.
Who'll come and care and protect children crying out for help?
We want to be children and to live in peace.

O Lord, focus me.
I've got so much homework to do,
I don't know where to start.
Tell me what to do first, second, third, and fourth
and how to plan better next time.

I don't know why I'm so angry and irritable.
God, I need a hug.

Lord, nothing is going right in my life.
I'm not doing well in school.
I don't have any friends.
My parents are fighting.
What am I going to do?
Please be my friend. I need You.

Come by here, my Lord.
I'm so scared today.
Mama's sick.
What will we do if she can't work?
Come by here, please, Lord.

Come by here, my Lord.
Daddy's drunk and angry,
and we are all very scared.
Come by here, please, Lord.

Come by here, my Lord.
My only friend doesn't like me anymore.
The children laugh at me,
and nobody plays with me.

Come by here, my Lord.
I want to die.
My daddy hurt me and made me
    feel bad.
Come by here, please, Lord.

Dear God,
Sometimes I want to be like
    everybody else—
so help me to be me.
Sometimes I want to act crazy,
so help me to keep my head.

Sometimes I want to try things
I know may hurt me and my parents,
so help me to think twice.
Sometimes I want to daydream
and not do my homework and chores,
so help me to be more disciplined.

Sometimes I just don't know
what I want to be and do,
so help me to be patient with me.

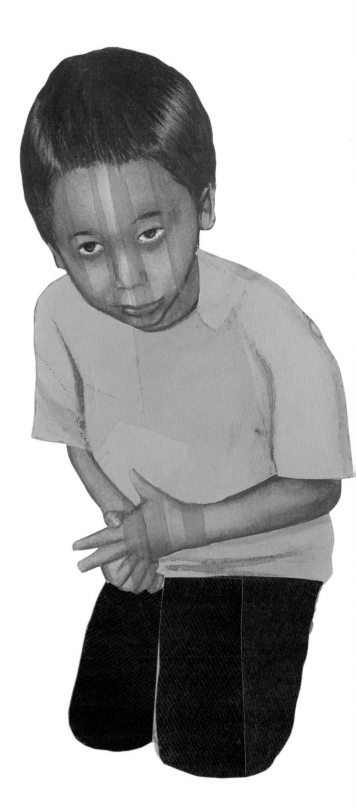

I'm down in the dumps today
and need You to lift me up.
Please send me a rainbow in the clouds,
so I can remember to sing and laugh
and be happy again.

PRAYER OF THANKS FOR PARENTS AND GRANDPARENTS AND ALL WHO CARE FOR CHILDREN

Lord,
There are so many kinds of parents.
I have a daddy and a mommy.
I have no daddy—just my mommy.
I have no mommy—just my daddy.
I have no mommy or daddy, but I have my grandmother.
I have two daddies and no mommy.
I have two mommies and no daddy.
My mommy is White and my daddy is Black.
My daddy is Asian and my mommy is Latina.
My parents can't speak English, walk, see, hear, or speak at all.
My parents are poor, but they work very hard to care for me.
Thank You for the special parents we have who love and care for us.
And that's what matters most.

PRAYER OF A LEARNING-DISABLED CHILD

Help me, Lord . . .

I read, but do not understand—even though I understand all I hear.

It's so hard to write—I can't share all I know in my head.

I know what I want to say in my mind,

but the words get all mixed up when I speak.

It's hard to sit still—it's like my motor is running too fast.

I pray for Your understanding and memory in my heart and mind.

Other kids think I'm stupid—and I sometimes feel like that myself.

Help me to keep trying, help my teachers to be patient,

and help the other kids to understand.

PRAYER OF A PHYSICALLY
CHALLENGED CHILD

Dear God,

I am blind, but can hear—no one has to shout.

(I am deaf but understand and can read with my eyes.)

(I cannot walk, but there is nothing wrong with my mind.)

I have a disability, and I am smart and have all the dreams anyone else has.

Help people to look at and see all of me and not just my challenge.

Help them to see what I can do, not what I can't.

A CHILD'S PRAYER ON
SEEING A PARENT ABUSED

God, please help our family.
My daddy hit my mommy and made her cry.
I wanted to help her
but I was too afraid.
My heart is bruised and broken.
I'll never forget what's happened.
Show us how to get the help we need to stop the hurting.

A FOSTER CHILD'S PRAYERS

Nobody remembered I was born today.
My daddy's in jail and
my mommy's an addict.
My grandma is sick, and
my aunt is so busy.
My sisters and brothers are scattered all over.
I've no one who cares, Lord, but know that You do.
Please send me a happy birthday card with love
all the way from Heaven above.

God,

I've survived twelve foster homes

I've been emotionally and physically abused

I've been all alone with no place to go.

No place to sleep.

No home to call my own.

No school that wants me.

No adults who claim me as their own.

In and out of detention.

Gone from dependent child

to delinquent child

to adult prisoner

on the treadmill of society's planned road to failure.

Nowhere else to go. No hope anywhere.

Nobody wants to know about me.

Nobody thinks I'm of any use.

Dispensable, disposable, invisible.

I'm just thrown away. Human garbage. Rejected.

God, will you cry with me?

PRAYER OF A CHILD IN DETENTION

God, where are you?

Why don't you hear me wailing

Moaning and groaning

I'm dying, dying, dying inside!

I'm in solitary detention. I've been beat up again.

They make me share a toothbrush and soap with

others. I can't breathe. I can't think.

I can't focus. I try not to feel

They yell at us and abuse us

and tell us we're no good.

Every day is hell. Every night is worse.

What is ahead for me, God?

Who will care?

Do you care, God?

If you do, please make the pain go away.

Please send me a ray of hope.

A GAY CHILD'S PRAYER

God,

I'm gay,

but I'm scared to say so.

My parents may be mad.

My grandparents may be sad.

My brother and sisters and friends may be ashamed of me.

My classmates may laugh at me and pick on me.

But You made me, Lord, and You love me, Lord.

Help me to accept myself and my feelings

and help other people to accept me, too.

A PRAYER FOR A FRIEND

Lord, why am I so different?
Why can't I be like all the other children?
I want to belong and to be somebody.
I wish I were prettier.
I wish I were cleverer.
I wish I were funnier.
I wish I had better clothes and lived in a better place.
I'm so lonely.
Please make me better.
Please send me a friend.

A DEPRESSED CHILD'S PRAYER

O God, I'm breaking into a million tiny pieces.
I don't think I can ever get back together again.
I'm so tired,
I can't get up.
I don't want to talk or think.
I don't want to hear anybody say anything
or have anybody look at me
or know anyone feels sorry for me.
I don't want to run anymore from my pain.
I just want it to go away forever.
I'm *so* alone and I'm *so* lonely.
Why doesn't anybody care?

Why should anybody care?
I'm worthless. I need help.
I need love.
I need a mother. I need a father.
I need someone—anyone—who cares just about me
so I don't have to be afraid anymore.
So I don't have to be alone anymore.
So I don't want to die anymore.
So I don't have to hurt and hurt inside
and keep praying the pain will go and stay away.
Please help me, God, escape this darkness
and learn to love and laugh and live again.

A DYING CHILD'S PRAYER

I am dying, Lord.
Help me not to be afraid
as I return home to You.
Send Your angels to pick me up and fly
me into Your loving and waiting arms.

Help my family, though they are sad,
to know that I am safe and happy with You
and that I'm glad my pain is over.
And tell them, Lord, that I will see them again
when You send Your angels back for them
when it is their time to share in Your new life.

A CHRISTIAN CHILD'S PRAYER FOR HEALING

Jesus healed the blind man
and helped him to see.
Jesus can heal me too.

Jesus healed the deaf man
and helped him to hear.
Jesus can heal me too.

Jesus healed the mute man
and helped him to talk.
Jesus can heal me too.

Jesus healed the lepers
and made their skins all new.
Jesus can heal me too.

Jesus stopped the woman's bleeding
and made her well again.
Jesus can heal me too.

Jesus chased away the crazed man's demons
and made him sane again.
Jesus can heal me too.

Jesus, please heal me too.

A CHILD'S PRAYER FOR A PARENT
DYING OF AIDS

Dear God in heaven,
My mother has AIDS
and will not live long,
and I will be all alone.
I am so afraid.
Will anyone want me?
Will anyone care for me?
Will anyone love me?
Will I get AIDS too and die soon?
Will You help me, God?

A PRAYER FOR AN OLDER CHILD ADDICTED TO
ALCOHOL, TOBACCO, OR OTHER DRUGS

God, I'm addicted to drugs and alcohol too.
I'm not myself but don't know what to do.
It feels so good for a little while, but
it feels so bad when the high wears off.
I want to escape, but I don't know how.
Help me, Lord, to get clean again so
I can be free of shame and depression
and live the life that You intend.

TRADITIONAL PRAYERS

THE LORD'S PRAYER

Our Father, who art in heaven,
hallowed be thy Name.

Thy kingdom come,
thy will be done,
on earth as it is in heaven.

Give us this day our daily bread.

And forgive us our trespasses,
as we forgive those who trespass against us.

And lead us not into temptation,
But deliver us from evil.

For thine is the kingdom, and the power, and the glory,
for ever and ever, Amen.

GRACES

Lord, we thank You for this food that we are about to receive for the
nourishment of our body in Christ's name. Amen.

Blessed art Thou, O Lord our God, King of the universe, who has brought
forth food from the earth. Amen.

DOXOLOGY

Praise God from Whom all blessings flow;
Praise Him all creatures here below;
Praise Him above, ye heavenly host;
Praise Father, Son, and Holy Ghost.

               —Thomas Ken, 1674

SELECTED PSALMS
NEW REVISED STANDARD VERSION

PSALM 8

O LORD, our Sovereign,
how majestic is your name
    in all the earth!
You have set your glory above the heavens.

Out of the mouths of babes
    and infants
      you have founded a bulwark
      because of your foes,
        to silence the enemy
        and the avenger.

When I look at your heavens,
    the work of your fingers,

the moon and the stars
      that you have established;

what are human beings that you
      are mindful of them,
mortals that you care for them?

Yet you have made them
      a little lower than God,
      and crowned them
      with glory and honor.

You have given them dominion
      over the works of your hands;
            you have put all things under
            their feet,

all sheep and oxen,
      and also the beasts of the field,

the birds of the air,
      and the fish
            of the sea,
      whatever passes along
            the paths of the seas.

O LORD, our Sovereign,
how majestic is your name
in all the earth!

PSALM 23

The LORD is my shepherd, I shall not want.

He makes me lie down in green pastures;
he leads me beside still waters;

he restores my soul.
He leads me in right paths
for his name's sake.

Even though I walk through the darkest valley,
I fear no evil;
for you are with me;
your rod and your staff—they comfort me.

You prepare a table before me
in the presence of my enemies;
you anoint my head
with oil;
my cup overflows.

Surely goodness and mercy
   shall follow me all the days of my life,
   and I shall dwell in the house of
   the LORD
   my whole life long.

PSALM 90

Lord, you have been our dwelling place
   in all generations.

Before the mountains were brought forth,
   or ever you had formed the earth and the world,
   from everlasting to everlasting you are God.

You turn us back to dust,
   and say, "Turn back,
   you mortals."

For a thousand years in your sight
   are like yesterday when it is past,
   or like a watch in the night.

You sweep them away;
   they are like a dream,
   like grass that is renewed

in the morning;

in the morning it flourishes
    and is renewed;
    in the evening it fades
    and withers.

For we are consumed by your anger;
    by your wrath we are overwhelmed.

You have set our iniquities before you,
    our secret sins in the light of your countenance.
For all our days pass away under your wrath;
    our years come to an end like a sigh.

The days of our life are seventy years, or perhaps eighty,
    if we are strong;
    even then their span is only toil and trouble;
    they are soon gone, and we fly away.

Who considers the power of your anger?
    Your wrath is as great as the fear
    that is due you.

So teach us to count our days
    that we may gain a wise heart.

Turn, O LORD! How long?
   Have compassion on your servants!

Satisfy us in the morning with your steadfast love,
   so that we may rejoice and be glad
   all our days.

Make us glad as many days
   as you have afflicted us,
   and as many years as we have seen evil.

Let your work be manifest to your servants,
   and your glorious power to their children.

Let the favor of the Lord our God be upon us,
   and prosper for us the work of our hands—
   O prosper the work of our hands!

PSALM 139
(verses 1—18)

O LORD, you have searched me
   and known me.

You know when I sit down
   and when I rise up;
   you discern my thoughts from far away.

You search out my path and my lying down,
 and are acquainted with all my ways.

Even before a word is on my tongue,
 O LORD, you know it completely.
You hem me in, behind and before,
 and lay your hand upon me.

Such knowledge is too wonderful for me;
 it is so high that I cannot attain it.

Where can I go from your spirit?
 Or where can I flee from your presence?

If I ascend to heaven,
 you are there;
 if I make my bed in Sheol,
 you are there.

If I take the wings of the morning
 and settle at the farthest limits of the sea,

even there your hand shall lead me,
 and your right hand shall hold me fast.

If I say, "Surely the darkness shall cover me,
 and the light around me become night,"

even the darkness is not dark to you;
    the night is as bright as the day,
    for darkness is as light to you.

For it was you who formed my inward parts;
    you knit me together in my mother's womb.

I praise you,
for I am fearfully and wonderfully made.
    Wonderful are your works;
    that I know very well.

My frame was not hidden from you,
    when I was being made in secret, intricately woven
    in the depths of the earth.

Your eyes beheld my unformed substance.
    In your book were written all the days
    that were formed for me,
    when none of them as yet existed.

How weighty to me are your thoughts,
    O God!
How vast is the sum of them!

I try to count them—they are more than the sand;
    I come to the end—I am still with you.

PRAYER FOR PEACE
A TWENTIETH-CENTURY PRAYER IN THE SPIRIT OF
SAINT FRANCIS OF ASSISI

Lord, make me an instrument of your peace.

Where there is hatred, let me sow love;

where there is injury, pardon;

where there is doubt, faith;

where there is despair, hope;

where there is darkness, light;

and where there is sadness, joy.

O Divine Master, grant that I may not so much seek

to be consoled as to console;

to be understood as to understand;

to be loved as to love.

For it is in giving that we receive;

it is in pardoning that we are pardoned;

and it is in dying that we are born to eternal life. Amen.

INDEX OF FIRST LINES